AWA IS FIGHTING DEPRESSION

AWA IS FIGHTING DEPRESSION

E.B. Kevin

Copyright © 2020 by E.B. Kevin.

Library of Congress Control Number:		2020903847
ISBN:	Hardcover	978-1-7960-8993-6
	Softcover	978-1-7960-8992-9
	eBook	978-1-7960-8991-2

All rights reserved. No part of this book may be reproduced or transmitted in any form or by any means, electronic or mechanical, including photocopying, recording, or by any information storage and retrieval system, without permission in writing from the copyright owner.

This is a work of fiction. Names, characters, places and incidents either are the product of the author's imagination or are used fictitiously, and any resemblance to any actual persons, living or dead, events, or locales is entirely coincidental.

Any people depicted in stock imagery provided by Getty Images are models, and such images are being used for illustrative purposes only.
Certain stock imagery © Getty Images.

Print information available on the last page.

Rev. date: 06/29/2020

To order additional copies of this book, contact:
Xlibris
1-888-795-4274
www.Xlibris.com
Orders@Xlibris.com
810151

CONTENTS

Dedication vii

Introduction ix
Awa Before Her Depression 1
Awa Is Depressed 25
Awa Overcomes Depression 53

Dedication

To my late grandfather, Theophilius Ernest Anin (T.E. Anin), who was a great author; to my mother, Stella Anin and my father, Kouadio Eyorekon Felix. To my brothers, Yannick, William, and Guy Benoit. To my friend, Rudolph Dadey who helped me overcome my depression. To all the people around the world who are fighting depression.

Introduction

According to the World Health Organization (WHO), depression is affecting over 264 million people worldwide. It's a mental health disorder that shouldn't be taken lightly and has serious effects on the body and one's mental health. It can cause fatigue, insomnia, weight loss, headaches, chronic pain and inflammation. It also brings about anxiety, mood swings, loss of motivation and energy, sadness, loneliness, isolation, suicidal thoughts, difficulty concentrating, negative thoughts, loss of appetite, hopelessness etc. But people who are depressed may not all experience the same symptoms. Some may experience more symptoms than others depending on the level of depression. The question is: should we blame people for being depressed? I don't think so. I remember a time when I was depressed for a few months and was actually surprised when it happened to me. I was living a happy life and thought I was too strong to be depressed. In fact, I didn't understand why some people were getting depressed; I thought they were too weak and I kept blaming them until I became depressed. I began to isolate myself and I was having suicidal thoughts. I became negative, I had no energy to do anything and had low self-esteem. Then I came to realise that nobody is exempt from this mental illness. Fortunately, I was able to overcome it afterwards and I learned a lot from my experience. Most of the time we judge or blame people without trying to find out what they are going through and the cause of their problems. Nobody wants to be depressed or chooses to be. Life is full of surprises, some good, some bad. People get depressed for different reasons. Financial worries, hardship, heartbreak, lack of affection, divorce, rejection, abuse, unemployment, grief from the death of a loved one, genetics, conflict, other illnesses, and personal issues can all lead to depression. Sometimes, some of the little things we take for granted may also lead to depression. What are those little things? Well, insults, unhappy relationships, smoking, alcohol addiction, unpleasant weather and even the city you live in. Living in a small and boring city where you don't know anyone may lead to depression.

Depression is a serious mental illness that should be tackled, and the purpose of this story is to help people who are depressed overcome their depression. The story is about a young woman called Awa who was living a normal life until the day she became depressed due to life events. The story is split into three parts. The first part focuses on Awa before she became depressed, the second part is about Awa being depressed and the last part of the story focuses on how she overcame her depression. Don't miss any part of the story. Perhaps, you are not depressed and might be telling yourself that you don't need to read this story. However, I strongly encourage you to read it even if you're not depressed. Why? Well, there may be people around you who are fighting depression and need your help. This story will enable you to help those people, and as I said before, no one is exempt from this mental illness so, it is crucial to know how to overcome it. On the other hand, if you are fighting depression, I guarantee that you'll be able to overcome it after reading this story.

Part 1

Awa Before Her Depression

Awa grew up in Ivory Coast with her parents and siblings. They all lived in Yopougon, a suburb in Abidjan also known as "Yop city." The official language in Ivory Coast is French. Awa was 21 years old and had 12 siblings (four brothers and eight sisters). This might surprise you, but it is common in African countries. African families are large and Africa is the continent with the highest fertility rate in the world. According to statistics, Africa has an average family size of 4.7 children per woman. *Back to the story!* Awa's father was a carpenter and her mother, unemployed. Unfortunately, they didn't have enough money to sponsor their children's education so, Awa and her siblings had never been to school. Their parents taught them how to read and write. Awa worked as a seamstress in a tailor shop in Yopougon. Her best friend Soraya taught her how to mend and make clothing. Both of them worked in the same tailor shop which belonged to Soraya's uncle and Soraya helped Awa get the job. Thanks to her job, Awa was able to earn a living and take care of herself. Awa was a very generous and hard-working woman and she used her salary to help her mother. She woke up at 6am every day and worked from 7am till 8pm, working 13 hours a day, from Monday to Saturday.

Awa had astounding seamstress skills which drew many customers to the tailor shop. She mended and made clothes quickly and effortlessly. She always met her customers' needs and expectations. Due to her seamstress skills, Awa became popular in her area and the whole suburb of Yopougon. Her customers recommended her to their relatives, acquaintances and friends. Soraya's uncle was very proud of Awa because she was contributing to his shop's success and growth. Awa was also very friendly and always welcomed her customers with a smile. She had a good relationship with them and never sounded or behaved like someone who had never been to school. She was smart, eloquent and had good manners. Her parents disciplined her when she was a kid and taught her well. They taught her to be independent so she wouldn't always rely on them or others emotionally, financially, nutritionally, mentally and psychologically. She learned to wash her clothes by herself, cook, clean, work etc.

Awa didn't have many friends; she always hung out with her best friend, Soraya, and considered her as her other half. They ate and drank together, exercised together, learned from each other and confided in one other. Awa and Soraya liked dancing so, they often went to a night club on Saturdays after work just to dance. Ivory Coast has a wide variety of music genres and dances. The most popular music genre in Ivory Coast is called *"Coupé-Décalé"* which means, "to cut and shift" in English. This music genre was created by a late Ivorian musician called Douk Saga. Young Ivorians love Coupé-Décalé and it is always played in night clubs and pubs. It was also Awa's favourite music genre. Although she was a hard-working person, she didn't underestimate the importance of having fun.

Awa believed in "working hard and playing hard." Having fun always helped her relieve stress and boost her mood, while spending fun moments with her best friend. Awa's mother always advised her to remain cautious and prudent anytime she went clubbing because Yopougon was not that safe at night. There were quite a number of robberies which occurred there at night. This was mainly due to unemployment, poverty, drug abuse and parental neglect. There were so many unemployed people in Yop City and they believed that the only way to feed themselves was by robbing other people at night. They often blamed the government for their unemployment which was sad and unfortunate because there should be no reason in the world to harm or do evil to others. Unemployment or poverty shouldn't lead people to do evil. No matter how hard life is, there is always a better solution.

Awa was aware of the unsafety of Yopougon, therefore, she was always cautious and prudent whenever she went clubbing with Soraya. Quite a number of men approached her when she went out, but she always rejected them. Awa was a pretty and virtuous woman so, she attracted many men. These men wanted to be in a relationship with her but she was not interested in any relationship. Awa wanted to be single for various reasons. First of all, she believed that being single would help her focus on her job and spend more time with her family and best friend. She understood that her parents didn't have enough money to take care of her, therefore, she took her job seriously and didn't want to lose it. Awa also thought that a boyfriend could get her pregnant and she was not ready to have a child. As far as she was concerned, having a child would entail lots of sacrifices. She wouldn't be able to work 13 hours a day if she had a child because she would have to take care of the child. She wouldn't have a social life until the child grows up. And according to her, it was costly to raise a child. She just wasn't mentally and financially prepared for it.

Moreover, Awa didn't want her children to go through hardship, suffering, and pain like she did. She wanted them to be educated unlike her, so she wanted to be financially prepared to be able to sponsor her children's education and offer them what she wished she had when she was a kid. She believed that her children must live better lives and achieve what she didn't achieve. Awa had always wanted to go to school to get a degree and even do a PhD, but her parents couldn't afford it. Awa's dream was to become a lawyer but she ended up being a seamstress because she had no educational background. She wanted her future children to go to the best schools and achieve their dreams and goals. Awa didn't want to make a mistake when choosing a life partner either so, she was very patient and careful about it. Her parents were pressuring her to get married and have kids but she told them she was not ready for it. They had even been looking for a life partner for her but Awa insisted that she preferred to be single for the moment. Her parents were quite disappointed in her but she had already made up her mind and stood by her decision.

Awa was a tough woman. She hardly changed her mind when she made a decision. Soraya was also like-minded. They both shared the same opinions and ideas. Soraya also didn't want to be in a relationship for the same reasons. That was part of the reason why both of them were best friends. Marriage is a big deal in Ivory Coast and in African culture. Most African parents want their children to marry at a young age for different reasons. Some think that marriage brings financial security into the family. They want their daughters to marry a wealthy man who will be able to take care of them financially and meet their needs and wants. Some want their children to marry in order to impress their friends, enemies, other relatives etc. Some African parents want their children to marry because they want to have grandchildren and others because they see marriage as a sign of happiness and success.

Awa's parents wanted her to get married to a rich man in order to bring financial security to the family. Awa was against their will and didn't consider the financial status of a man as a requirement to look for in a life partner. She didn't want to be financially dependent on her future husband. She believed that a wife should be financially independent. According to Awa, when a wife is financially dependent on her husband, it gives more power and control to him. He can even lose respect for her and manipulate her. And if the marriage doesn't work and they divorce, the wife would suffer financially. Therefore, Awa worked hard in order to have financial freedom and security. She was planning to get a better job in the future because her salary was not enough for her to build her own house or even rent a studio or an apartment. Therefore, she still lived with her parents and siblings. Awa wanted to be wealthy to be able to take care of her whole family. She wanted the best for her family and was willing to pay the price for it.

Awa was the youngest among all her siblings but she worked harder than them and became the only one among them who had a job. Unfortunately, all her siblings were unemployed. It was difficult for them to find jobs because they had no degrees. Awa was just lucky to have a job thanks to her friend, Soraya. Awa's father, Suleiman, used his salary and savings to feed Awa's siblings. He was 70 years old but still worked to be able to take care of his children. He didn't want to retire until Awa's siblings had all become financially independent. Suleiman loved his children so much and basically lived for them. He wasn't wealthy, but was full of knowledge and wisdom. According to him, knowledge was the greatest wealth in life and being knowledgeable was equal to being successful. He valued the importance of money but believed that knowledge was more important than money. Suleiman had a close relationship with all his children and always taught them life lessons based on his life experiences. He was his children's mentor and, he liked spending time with them when he wasn't at work. Every evening, Suleiman and his family would gather for dinner. His wife, Aisha cooked delicious Ivorian dishes and the whole family loved her food. There is a wide variety of dishes in Ivory Coast. The most popular Ivorian dish is "Attiéké au poisson," which is cassava and fish in English. Awa's family loved attiéké au poisson and Aisha cooked it perfectly. She also taught her daughters how to cook so that they could cook for their future husbands and kids. It's also part of the African culture, most African mothers teach their daughters how to cook from a young age. Awa learned to cook when she was seven years old.

In Ivory Coast, cooking is a crucial skill that a woman needs and women who know how to cook are respected and appreciated in the country. Ivorians love food and most of them eat four times a day. They'd have breakfast, lunch, "goûter" and dinner in a day. "Goûter" means a snack which they usually have around 4pm. Snacks are sold in the streets at cheap prices and 773.10 CFA Franc is usually more than enough to buy a meal or snacks in Ivory Coast. The Ivorian's currency is the CFA Franc (XOF) and 773.10 CFA Franc (XOF) equates to 1 pound sterling (GBP). A 773.10 CFA Franc meal is a filling and solid meal in Ivory Coast. Food is affordable in Ivory Coast therefore, Awa and her family were able to feed themselves properly on a daily basis despite their low financial status. They never lacked sufficient food. Awa and Aisha went to the market three times a month to buy groceries for the house. Although their house was very small for the whole family, they were able to cope with it. They were 15 in total (13 siblings, two parents) and they all lived in a 3-bedroom house. Awa's parents had their own room. Awa and four of her sisters shared the same room, her other four sisters slept in the living room and her four brothers shared the other room. They weren't living in good conditions but were grateful for what they had. At least they had a house to live in and were not homeless. As far as they were concerned, it was much better to live with many people in a house than to be homeless. Awa's family was very united and loving. They argued at times but still loved one another a lot. They had different opinions and ideas but never judged one another.

Awa's brothers were protective of their sisters. They often accompanied them when they went out due to the young robbers in their area. They didn't want them to get robbed or abused. Several girls in the area had been victims of robbery and sexual assaults and the police weren't taking any action against it. Therefore, the robbers felt untouchable. Awa's brothers worked out every day, as they enjoyed building muscles. Therefore, they were very strong and muscular. They were also very tall and the robbers in their area were all afraid of them. Awa and her sisters felt safe hanging around their brothers. In addition, Suleiman told his sons to watch over their sisters due to the unsafety in their area. He cared so much for his family and didn't want anything bad to happen to them. However, Awa and her sisters also liked freedom. They didn't always want to be surrounded by their brothers, especially when they went out with their friends. Therefore, their brothers were not always with them when they went out.

Soraya's uncle, Jeremiah, had been treating Awa like his daughter due to her good behaviour and excellent work at his tailor shop. He had been making more profits since she started working with him so, he wanted to appoint her as the manager of the shop. However, Awa didn't know about it because it was meant to be a surprise. Soraya, who was Jeremiah's personal assistant, was very happy to hear that her uncle wanted to appoint Awa as the manager of the tailor shop. Awa's monthly salary was 77622.24 CFA franc (£100) and her new position would help her earn a better salary. The average salary of a tailor or seamstress in Ivory Coast is about 47463.93 CFA franc a month (£64.42). This salary can do very little in Europe and most parts of the world but can allow a person to feed themselves for one month in Ivory Coast, even though it is still not enough to become financially independent. Notwithstanding, Awa was going to earn 589600.92 CFA franc a month (£800) if she got the managerial position, which would allow her to help her mother more as well as her siblings. Jeremiah issued Awa's contract and reserved the necessary funds to pay her monthly.

Soraya and Jeremiah planned to prank Awa before informing her of her promotion. So, they decided to make her think she was going to be fired and that they had found someone to replace her. A few days later, Awa arrived at work early in the morning and Jeremiah asked her to come to his office to have a serious conversation. Jeremiah usually talked to Awa with a smile on his face but this time, he looked angry and even frowned. Awa was a bit nervous and scared because she had never seen him frowning and being that angry. She thought she did something wrong and didn't understand what was really going on. Soraya was also in the office with them. She also frowned and looked angry. Then Jeremiah told Awa that she was fired and should leave the shop as soon as possible, and that he already found someone else to replace her. Awa was so shocked and began to weep, because she felt she had lost everything and she asked Jeremiah why he fired her. Jeremiah claimed that it was time for her to leave the shop as he had found someone who had greater seamstress skills and was more qualified. Awa continued to weep and Soraya did not show any empathy.

As she was about to leave Jeremiah's office, Jeremiah called her back to tell her that it was a prank; she had not been fired but was rather promoted to a manager's role. He told her that he wanted her to be the manager of his tailor shop due to her incredible seamstress skills and ability to attract more customers. Awa had great marketing skills too. He told her that he was very happy with her performance and gave her a new contract. Awa then stopped weeping and began to rejoice. She couldn't believe what was going on. She became extremely excited and glad about it. Soraya rejoiced with her and told her that she deserved this promotion. Awa thanked Soraya and Jeremiah with so much gratefulness in her heart, and read her contract. As she was reading it, she saw her new salary (589600.92 CFA franc) and was even more excited. She kept on smiling and then signed her new contract. She thanked them one more time. She told Jeremiah that he could count on her for this manager's role, that she would perform even better and work harder to help him make more profits. Jeremiah was happy to hear that and told Awa how he had absolute trust in her and strongly believed that she would fulfil her managerial tasks effectively.

Awa and Soraya decided to have a drink together after work to celebrate Awa's promotion. They went to an Ivorian restaurant called "Jardin d'Eden" which means "the Garden of Eden" in English. It is a popular restaurant in Abidjan located in an area called "Riviera 3." When they arrived at the restaurant, Soraya ordered a bottle of champagne for her and Awa. Awa said that she couldn't afford it but Soraya told her not to worry about it, that she would pay for the bottle. Awa thanked her and told her that she appreciates her kindness and they would remain best friends for life. At some point, Awa asked Soraya to tell her more about the whole story and the process of how her uncle had decided to promote her. Soraya began to laugh and told the whole story to Awa, about how Jeremiah informed her that he would give Awa a manager's role but wanted to prank her before telling her about it. Awa started laughing and teasing Soraya that she should have told her earlier on. She said she was so scared and sad when she heard that she was fired, she felt that was the end of her life. Soraya told her that her uncle would never fire her, that he liked her and appreciated the work she had been doing at the tailor shop. The restaurant's waiter brought the bottle of champagne and Awa and Soraya drank it to celebrate the promotion. Awa said that she couldn't wait to announce the good news to her family members, especially her mother, because she loved her with all her heart. She also said her new salary would allow her to financially support her family. Her mother wanted to start a home hairdressing business and Awa said she would be able to help her buy the necessary equipment for the business. Awa's new salary is considered to be a good salary in Abidjan as you can do much with it there. Awa thanked Soraya one more time, and Soraya advised her on how she should go about her new manager's role in order to fulfil her tasks and please Jeremiah. She told her to continue to work hard and provide exceptional services to customers. Awa listened carefully to Soraya and promised to follow her advice.

After having a drink with Soraya, Awa went home and announced the good news to all her family members. Her family was really happy for her and Aisha began to sing an Ivorian song and ran towards Awa to hug her tightly. Suleiman began to weep for joy and also hugged Awa and told her how proud and happy he was. Surprisingly, two of her sisters, Fatou and Myriam, looked unhappy about Awa's promotion. They frowned and didn't say a word. Everyone else in the house noticed their strange behaviours and attitudes but they didn't mind them. They rather focused on the good news. It was 10pm and Aisha cooked Awa's favourite meal to celebrate her promotion (it's never too late to have dinner). Awa and her family had dinner together except Fatou and Myriam. Both of them were so furious and jealous that they went to sleep whilst the others were celebrating. Awa promised her mother that she was going to help her start her home hairdressing business. Aisha rejoiced even more and thanked Awa. She even rolled on the floor and sang a song of joy. Ivorians and most African mothers like to roll on the floor when they're extremely happy about something. Furthermore, Awa said that her salary wasn't that much to take care of all her 12 siblings but she will do her best to support them. She promised to save some money to help some of her siblings start a small business to earn a living. Her siblings were all happy to hear Awa's promise and didn't stop thanking her. Then they all went to sleep after the dinner.

The following day, Awa woke up early in the morning as usual and went to work in a good mood. Fatou and Myriam were still angry and gossiped about Awa the whole day. They felt Awa was more appreciated and loved in the family. They said that Awa was the only lucky person among her siblings as she was the only one who had a job among them. They felt isolated and unlucky. They were jealous of Awa because they were unemployed. They wished that they had a job like her. On the other hand, Awa began her new manager's role and worked hard during the whole day. There were exactly 10 seamstresses and tailors excluding Awa and Soraya at Jeremiah's tailor shop and Awa was managing all of them. Jeremiah barely went to work because he was the CEO of the shop and he didn't mend or make clothing. He had other tasks. He handled the financial activities of the shop, financial statements and the procurement. He purchased all the materials and equipment for the shop. Awa understood all her managerial tasks and was able to fulfil all of them on a daily basis. Even though she got a new position, she was still humble and worked even harder. She treated the other employees fairly and nicely but she was a bit tough on them to push them to get the work done properly and faster. She understood that as a manager she also had to be quite tough on employees for them to respect her and work as they should. Awa enjoyed her new role and was able to grow the business even more through her amazing skills and talents. The tailor shop experienced profit growth and customer growth since Awa became the manager of the shop. Soraya and Jeremiah were very impressed and congratulated Awa for her good job. All the tailor shop employees liked Awa and had a good relationship with her. Awa believed that a manager should be close to employees and make them feel good so as to get the best out of them. It was amazing to see how Awa understood management and marketing strategies, although she had never been to school. This proves that someone can be smart without a degree or an education. This modern society tends to look down on people who are not educated and don't have a degree but it is possible to be smart without a degree.

At the end of the month, Awa received her new salary directly into her bank account and was really happy about it. She used her salary to buy hairdressing equipment for her mother as promised. She bought shampoo, scissors, mirrors, chairs, a hairdryer, tongs, towels, gowns, a comb etc. She also made flyers to distribute them to people in her area in order to attract customers. All the equipment and flyers cost her 120000.00 CFA Francs which is equivalent to around 154.39 pounds sterling. *Currencies fluctuate so it might not be the same equivalence when you'll be reading this book.* Anyway, Awa brought all the equipment home and gave them to her mother. Aisha was so happy and thanked her daughter. They decided to use the living room as a salon and remove the hairdressing equipment in the evenings to allow those who sleep in the living room to sleep at night. Aisha and Awa began to distribute the flyers in their area and from door to door. Luckily enough, Aisha started having customers a few days after. The customers were all happy about the price which was 7400 CFA Francs per person (about £10.06). It was way cheaper than other salons. Customers were also satisfied with Aisha's services. She was meeting their needs and expectations. She styled their hair nicely and was kind to them. Awa taught her some marketing strategies and told her to build a relationship with her customers. Aisha continued to attract more customers and made about 111000.00 CFA Francs a day as she had about 15 customers a day. Awa was so happy about it and didn't regret supporting her mother financially. Aisha was able to financially support her children with her income. Suleiman was also happy about it and advised Aisha to save some money to open a salon in the area so that the family can have more space in the house and that it will be more convenient for customers as well. Aisha agreed with him and began to save money to open a salon in their area. He also asked her to employ her daughters so that they could help her and earn a living as well. Aisha liked the idea and agreed with Suleiman.

One year later, Aisha opened a salon in Yopougon and employed her daughters including Fatou and Myriam. Fatou and Myriam were happy to work with their mother because they had always wanted to work in order to earn a living like Awa. They were no longer jealous of Awa because they had found a job. Aisha increased her price to 15000 CFA Francs to be able to pay the salon bills and her daughters. Customers were still coming to the salon and were more comfortable in it. There were fans and more equipment in the salon. On the other hand, there wasn't any fan in her living room where she was doing her hairdressing business and customers had felt very hot over there. However, they were all happy that there were fans in her new salon. It is really hot in Abidjan, therefore, it's very crucial to have a fan or an air conditioner at home and in other locations. Due to her new salon, Aisha became very popular in Yopougon and her daughters have been able to earn a living and become financially independent. Suleiman couldn't believe what had happened to his family and was really proud of his wife and especially Awa. Aisha thanked Awa all the time because she had helped her start her business; she acknowledged that she couldn't have achieved this if Awa hadn't financially supported her. Awa focused on helping her brothers since Aisha was helping her sisters. She saved enough money to open a newspaper shop to allow her brothers to work and earn a living. They worked from Monday to Saturday and sold newspapers to people in Yopougon. They liked their jobs and became financially independent. Suleiman was happy that all his family members were working and had become financially independent. He was now 71 years old and wanted to retire as he was only working to financially support his family. He felt it was time for him to retire and rest. However, Awa felt it was time to move to her own studio and live on her own, so she moved out from her parents' house after some time. Her siblings did the same as they were all earning a monthly income and could afford to rent a studio. They all considered Awa as a role model and followed in her footsteps. All of them found a studio in Yopougon and Awa's parents were now living by themselves in their house. They were sad to see their children leave their house but were happy at the same time to see them become financially independent. Nevertheless, the whole family always met at Suleiman's house on the weekends to spend time together.

Awa was very happy about all the good things that happened to her family. She had played a big role in her family. Her new manager's role had a big positive impact on all of them. Due to her promotion, her mother and all her siblings were now working and had become financially independent without degrees or an education. Suleiman retired and now spent all his time at home. He continued to advise his children and wanted all of them to get married and have a family. None of his children were married yet. Awa told Soraya about everything that happened in her family and Soraya was so happy about it. She said to Awa: "this is just the beginning and there is more to come."

This looks like the end of the story but no, the story continues. Let's move to part 2.

Part 2

Awa Is Depressed

What happened to Awa's family was unbelievable. Awa became a manager, Aisha became a successful hairdresser, Awa's siblings got a job and became financially independent. Suleiman retired and was proud of his whole family, especially Awa. It's a wonder! Awa continued to make an impact at the tailor shop with her astounding managerial and marketing skills. People were amazed to see someone who had never been to school having such skills and intelligence. They even found it difficult to believe that she had never been to school. She was smarter and more skillful than many educated people who had a degree. Soraya always said good things about Awa to everyone and was proud to have her as her best friend. Awa and Soraya had been friends for 14 years and Soraya was two years older than her. Both of them enjoyed working in the same tailor shop. It helped them see each other from Monday to Saturday and they went out after work sometimes.

One day, Jeremiah called Awa into his office and asked her to sit on the office chair. Soraya was working in her office at that time. Jeremiah began to talk to Awa in an unusual manner. He said to Awa, "I like your outfit, you look so pretty." Awa looked confused and shocked at the same time as she didn't expect that from him. She felt shy and was looking down at the floor. Jeremiah continued to flirt with her and asked her whether she was single. Nonetheless, Jeremiah was married to a woman called Carole (Soraya's aunt) and they had been married for 35 years. Awa kept quiet for a few minutes and asked Jeremiah why he had asked her that question. Jeremiah said he was just curious to know the answer. Then, Awa told him that she was single.

Jeremiah looked happy when he heard that and didn't stop smiling. He noticed that Awa was feeling shy and nervous but he didn't stop flirting with her. He asked her to relax and told her that everything was fine, and began to touch her hair. Awa was shivering as she saw him as a father and didn't expect him to act this way towards her. She asked him to stop it as she knew his intentions. Jeremiah asked her to relax one more time and held her hands. He said to her, "I will give you whatever you want if you agree to be with me. I will even double your salary."

Awa replied: "no, you are the head of the tailor shop and my best friend's uncle. I can't do that. And you are much older than me, you are like a father to me." Jeremiah didn't mind her at all, and forcefully kissed her. As he was kissing her, Soraya came into his office and saw what was happening.

Soraya shouted, "what…" and Jeremiah immediately stopped kissing Awa. Awa tried to explain to Soraya what had happened and told her that he was forcing himself on her. Soraya didn't believe Awa and was so disappointed in her; she looked very upset and left the office instantly. Jeremiah didn't say a word, he didn't defend Awa neither did he explain what had really happened. Awa felt so embarrassed and started crying. The other employees saw Soraya leaving the office upset and heard Awa cry, but they did not really know what was happening.

Awa said to Jeremiah, "It's your fault, why did you forcefully kiss me? I asked you to stop it but you didn't listen to me. Now my best friend thinks I am your mistress and she's angry at me. I considered you as a father but you proved me wrong."

Jeremiah replied, "calm down Awa, I will sort it out. Stop crying. I have feelings for you and I thought it was time for you to know about it. Don't worry about your friendship with Soraya, I will talk to her when I get home. But I am giving you time to think about what I said to you. I really like you and I still want to be with you." Awa was upset to hear that and left the office immediately. She tried to reach Soraya on the phone to convince her that it wasn't her fault, but Soraya was not picking up her calls. Awa went to Soraya's house and knocked on her door, but Soraya didn't open the door as she knew it was Awa. Awa went home disappointed and sad. She felt that this was the end of her friendship with Soraya. Jeremiah went to his house in the evening and met Soraya and she frowned at him. Jeremiah apologized to her and told her that it was just an accident. He didn't tell her that he forcefully kissed Awa though.

Soraya didn't believe him and said to him, "how can you kiss my best friend? She's much younger than you. Aren't you ashamed of yourself? She's also your employee. How can you kiss your employee? I am very disappointed in you Uncle, and I want you to fire Awa. I don't want to be her friend anymore. She just betrayed me and I am so disappointed in her. I thought she was my best friend but I consider her as my enemy now. Please fire her, I don't want to see her at the tailor shop any longer."

Jeremiah replied, "calm down Soraya, Awa is your best friend and a good manager. She has helped the shop make more profits and I can't fire her like that. She doesn't deserve to be fired. I think you should forgive her and continue to be friends with her."

Soraya replied, "Uncle, I can't be friends with her anymore. Fire her or else I will tell Auntie that you cheated on her." Soraya went to her room and slammed the door angrily. Jeremiah was so afraid when she said that she was going to tell his wife that he cheated on her. He even had a sleepless night after arguing with his niece as he thought about it the whole night. His wife, Carole, was not at home when Jeremiah and Soraya were arguing and she had no idea what was happening.

The following day, Awa went to work early in the morning and met Soraya at the tailor shop's reception. She tried to talk to Soraya and told her the truth about what had happened in Jeremiah's office but Soraya didn't mind her and went straight to her office and closed the door. Awa went to work as she didn't want to bother Soraya or other people in the shop. During the day, Soraya began to treat Awa differently. She was rude to her and complained about everything she was doing even though Awa was doing her job properly. Awa couldn't believe what was happening, she had never seen Soraya behave this way before. Soraya had turned into a completely different person, she was naughty and intolerable. She was trying to make Awa uncomfortable to push her to step down. Jeremiah came to the tailor shop in the afternoon and noticed that Awa was feeling sad and hopeless. He asked her what was happening and she told him that because of what he did to her, his niece was disrespecting her and treating her badly.

Jeremiah went to Soraya's office and asked her, "why are you being disrespectful towards Awa?"

Soraya replied, "Uncle, are you defending her now? Do you like her more than me?"

Jeremiah replied, "oh stop it Soraya, don't try to manipulate me. You know that I like you more than her, you are my beloved niece, but I just want you to respect her and treat her fairly like you used to. Don't forget that she's the manager of this shop and we need her."

Soraya replied, "I don't care if she's the manager. I helped her get a job in this shop before she even became the manager. What are you waiting for to fire her? I give you one more day to make a decision about it or else Auntie will know what happened between you and Awa." Jeremiah asked her to calm down and forget about what happened and move on. He told her that if she really wants him to stay married to her aunt, she shouldn't tell her what happened between him and Awa. Soraya said that she didn't care, she just wanted him to fire Awa. Jeremiah went back to his office as he didn't know what to do. He was very confused.

Awa continued to work although she wasn't feeling good because of Soraya's behavior towards her and what Jeremiah did to her. Jeremiah called her into his office again but she was afraid to go there as she thought he would do the same thing to her again. She told him that she will only come to his office if he wants to discuss office work and nothing else. Jeremiah had bad intentions and still wanted to flirt with Awa despite what had happened. Awa didn't mind him and focused on her work. She asked him to stop flirting with her and told him that she was not interested in having a relationship with him. She told him to tell the truth to Soraya so that they will be best friends again.

Luckily enough Jeremiah got angry and said to her, "If you don't want to be in a relationship with me, I will fire you."

Awa looked shocked and cried again. She felt she was going to lose her job and become unemployed. She loved her job and didn't want to lose it. She needed her salary to pay her rent, bills, and take care of herself. She had worked at the tailor shop for several years and was emotionally attached to it. She then said to Jeremiah, "you are married and I don't have feelings for you. You are much older than me and you are my boss. My friendship with Soraya has ended because of you and my only wish is to have her back. One more time, I can never be in a relationship with you. I am here to work and not to seek love."

Jeremiah replied, "Awa, I give you one day to think about it or else you will be fired." Awa cried even more and could no longer focus on her work. Later in the evening, she went to talk to her parents about everything that had happened between her and Jeremiah.

Suleiman was upset when Awa told him what Jeremiah had done to her at work. He said that he was going to go to his house to beat him up and warn him to leave Awa alone. Suleiman had liked to fight when he was younger and had taken karate classes. Aisha was also so disappointed in Jeremiah as she had thought he was a good person. She asked her husband to calm down but he didn't listen to her and went straight to Jeremiah's house. He also asked Awa to come along. Awa was afraid and thought it was a bad idea as this could affect her job and make Soraya hate her more. Suleiman was uncontrollable when upset, so she couldn't calm him down. He was very protective of his children, especially his daughters. It was 10pm, and Suleiman and Awa arrived at Jeremiah's house. Suleiman angrily knocked on Jeremiah's door and shouted his name, "Jeremiah… open the door."

Jeremiah was afraid and thought there were armed robbers in front of his house. He shouted, "who is it? Don't break my door…"

Suleiman replied, "I am Awa's father. Open the door…." Jeremiah was surprised as it was too late and he wasn't expecting anyone at home. He opened the door and saw Awa with Suleiman. He was afraid when he saw Awa and he immediately knew that she had told her father about what he did to her. He became very nervous when he saw them. Suleiman shouted at him, "why did you forcefully kiss my daughter? Is there something wrong with you?"

Jeremiah tried to deny it but Awa said to her dad, "Daddy, he's lying. He did it and now he's threatening to fire me if I don't get into a relationship with him."

Jeremiah replied, "I am sorry Suleiman, please forgive me. We are all humans and we all make mistakes."

Suleiman replied, "why did you lie? I am warning you to leave my daughter alone and never kiss her again. You are too old for her. And stop threatening to fire her if she doesn't get into a relationship with you."

Jeremiah replied, "okay." Suddenly, Suleiman slapped Jeremiah so hard that Carole and Soraya heard it in their respective rooms. *"A former carpenter's palms are hard. Can you imagine?"* It all happened in front of Jeremiah's house and Carole and Soraya were sleeping in their respective rooms so they didn't know what was happening until they heard the sound of a slap. Both of them came out of their rooms to find out what was happening and they saw Awa, Suleiman and Jeremiah in front of the house. Jeremiah was still recovering from the slap he had received from Suleiman and was completely quiet. Soraya knew what was happening when she saw them but Carole had no idea what was going on. Soraya didn't even greet Awa when she saw her as she was still angry at her but Carole greeted Awa and Suleiman. She knew them well; she had met them at their house when Soraya was still friends with Awa.

Carole asked Suleiman what was going on and Suleiman replied instantly, "your husband forcefully kissed my daughter at work and threatened to fire her if she didn't get into a relationship with him."

Carole was extremely shocked and couldn't believe it, she asked him, "are you sure of what you are saying?"

Suleiman replied, "you should rather ask your husband whether it's true."

Carole asked Jeremiah, "Is it true that you forcefully kissed Awa at work and threatened to fire her if she doesn't get into a relationship with you?"

Jeremiah replied, "yes, but I am sorry, forgive me Carole."

Carole asked Awa as well, "did my husband really do that to you?"

Awa hesitated and said, "yes, he did." Carole was so disappointed in Jeremiah and told him that their marriage was over, that she wanted to divorce him. She felt embarrassed that her husband did that to Awa as she loved her and considered her as her daughter. Jeremiah begged Carole for forgiveness but she refused it and insisted on divorcing him. Soraya began to cry and went straight to her room. Remember she had threatened her uncle to report him to Carole if he didn't fire Awa but she was now sad to hear that they were going to divorce. Suleiman and Awa went back home late and Jeremiah and Carole were arguing in their living room. Soraya locked herself in her room and continued to cry in there. Jeremiah went to knock on her door but she refused to open it.

The following day, Soraya told Jeremiah to fire Awa straight away. She hated her more because she felt they were going to divorce because of her even though it wasn't Awa's fault. This time, Jeremiah agreed to fire Awa because her father had slapped him and reported him to his wife the night before. Awa went to work the same day and as she was working, Jeremiah went into her office to tell her that she's being fired and she should leave the office as soon as possible. Awa asked him why he fired her but he didn't reply and walked away. He was so furious. Awa began to cry and went to tell all the other employees in the tailor shop that she was fired and this was her last day at work. They were all sad and couldn't believe it as Awa was a great manager and was performing well. They asked her the reason why Jeremiah fired her but she didn't want to tell them the whole story. She preferred to keep it to herself. On the other hand, Soraya was glad to hear that Awa was fired as she didn't want to see her any longer.

Awa went to her studio afterwards and couldn't stop crying; she remembered all the good times she had spent at the tailor shop, how she got her first job and became a manager, all the good moments she had spent with Soraya and how their friendship had ended. She remembered what she was able to do with her salary, how she had financially supported her mother and siblings and helped them become financially independent. Awa lost her job, her best friend and her joy. She called her parents to tell them that she lost her job and they were also sad and disappointed. They also cried and tried to comfort her but she was totally inconsolable. Awa became depressed. She had a sleepless night and felt like ending her life. She had suicidal thoughts and isolated herself in her studio. To her big surprise, her siblings did not feel sad when they heard that she had lost her job. They were rather happy and this shocked her and made her feel more depressed. She couldn't believe that the people she had helped in the past were now turning their backs on her. Her best friend and siblings had rejected her.

Awa then stopped going out; she was always in her studio from morning to evening and had no interest and motivation to do anything. She even lost weight as she barely ate and spent all her time in bed by herself. Her depression was getting worse every day and her parents were worried. They never thought that this could happen to her as she was always happy and proactive. Awa was spreading happiness wherever she went and liked being surrounded by people. She was very sociable but her depression turned her into an antisocial person. She was always by herself and the only people that remained faithful to her were her parents. They visited her regularly to check up on her and give her food to eat. Aisha cooked for her but she had completely lost her appetite. Awa's parents were disappointed in Awa's siblings, they couldn't believe that they were rejecting Awa and didn't even bother to visit her to find out how she was doing. They thought they knew their children, but Awa's situation made her realise how much they didn't know them. In fact, Awa's situation revealed the true character of her siblings. *"Sometimes, it's not the people who change, it's the mask that falls off."*

Suleiman and Aisha advised them but nothing had changed. They still didn't visit Awa and acted like they didn't know her and that she was not part of their family. They forgot that Awa had financially supported them and was always there for them when they needed her. *We live in such an evil world.* Fortunately, Awa had saved some money while she had been working at the tailor shop, therefore, she was able to pay her rent and studio bills for some time. Her mother told her that she was going to financially support her if she ran out of money. She even suggested that she works with her at her salon, but Awa was too depressed to work and was not interested in the offer. In addition, Awa's sisters didn't want her to work with them at the salon.

Awa lost her confidence and had insomnia every night. She was always thinking about death and became very pessimistic. She used to be very optimistic and full of life but her depression highly affected her. Suleiman and Aisha were afraid that she might commit suicide one day, therefore, they asked her to move out of her studio and come and live with them. They felt less worried living with her and thought she shouldn't be living by herself due to her depression. Awa moved out of her studio and went to live in her parents' house. Notwithstanding, she was still depressed and was always in her room. She even lost more weight. Her mother forced her to eat more but she had no appetite. Awa felt weak and was experiencing extreme fatigue. Aisha bought some antidepressants for her but they all seemed not to be working for her. Awa was still depressed and still felt lonely even though she was living with her parents. She also felt irritated on a daily basis and didn't feel like talking to anyone. She thought she was never going to make it in life and that she was stupid. She used to have brilliant dreams and ambitions but ended up not believing in any of them. She didn't see any point in living any longer. She missed Soraya as both of them had been best friends and shared similar ideas, opinions, interests and had lots of things in common. Moreover, Soraya had not tried to reach out to Awa since the day she was fired. She completely forgot about her and acted like they were never best friends before. On the other hand, Jeremiah and Carole divorced a few weeks after Carole found out what her husband had done to Awa. Carole moved out to Cocody, a suburb in Abidjan, and Soraya spent the weekends with her.

Three months later, Awa's father experienced weight loss, itchy skin, fatigue and felt sick. Aisha sent him to the hospital for a check-up. After a few weeks, the doctor called him to come and collect his test results. Suleiman went to the hospital with Aisha and he was diagnosed with liver cancer. Surprisingly, he wasn't feeling sad and told his wife and the doctor that he was not afraid of death because of his age. Aisha cried when she heard that he had cancer. Suleiman asked her to stop crying and told her that even if he passed away, it would be the will of God. The doctor asked him to go for a surgery but Suleiman couldn't afford it. Nevertheless, Aisha said she was going to use all her savings from her hairdressing business to pay for the surgery. Suleiman thanked Aisha and agreed to go for a surgery. He scheduled a doctor's appointment for the surgery and went back home with Aisha. Aisha was very sad and both of them didn't know how to announce the sad news to their children, especially Awa, because of what she was going through. When they arrived home, Suleiman went into Awa's room to announce the sad news to her but she was asleep. He was even surprised to find her asleep as she had been having insomnia since her depression started. He then went to his room and decided to wait until she wakes up to tell her about his test results.

He went back to her room the following day and found her in bed listening to a sad song. He felt even sadder but asked her to come to the living room to have a chat with him. Awa agreed and went to the living room with her dad. Both of them sat and watched TV, and as they were talking, Suleiman told her that he had been to see the doctor and unfortunately, he had been diagnosed with liver cancer. Awa began to shout, "what…" and couldn't believe it. She cried and felt more depressed. She was saying, "Dad, I don't want you to die, I love you so much and I need you to stay by my side."

Suleiman replied, "Awa don't worry, I will go for a surgery in a few weeks and I will be fine. Stop crying." Awa was still worried and went back to her room sad and demoralised. It was just too much for her to bear; she had lost her best friend, her job and now her father was diagnosed with liver cancer. She became more pessimistic and had more suicidal thoughts.

Aisha tried to comfort her when she came back from work but Awa was still inconsolable. Suleiman told his other children that he was diagnosed with liver cancer and they were also sad. They were all afraid to lose their father.

A few weeks later, Suleiman went to the hospital for his surgery. He wasn't nervous but his wife and children were. Before the surgery he said to Aisha: "If I die during the surgery, tell our children that I love them all and they should be united, follow all the advice I gave them, and love one another." He further asked Aisha to take good care of Awa and help her overcome her depression, and he told her that he loved her with all his heart and he thanked her for everything she had done for him since the beginning of the day they met. Aisha hugged him tightly and began to cry. She told him that she loved him too and was grateful for everything he had done for her and their children.

She said to him, "you are the best husband and father in the world. I love you so much my darling. I believe your surgery will be successful and we will celebrate it with our children when you recover from it." Aisha had hope and Suleiman hoped for the best but was prepared for the worst. After talking to Aisha, Suleiman went to the operation room for his surgery. Aisha waited at the hospital reception and was very nervous and anxious. She was shivering and couldn't wait for the surgery to finish. She kept on asking the receptionist whether the surgery was still going on and what time it will finish. The receptionist told her to calm down and that the doctor will inform her when the surgery is over, that she had no idea what was going on at the moment as she had no access to the operating room. Aisha was so impatient and couldn't stop walking up and down the hospital reception. She even began to sweat at some point. The surgery took about 5 hours but unfortunately, Suleiman died during the surgery. The doctor didn't know how to announce it to Aisha. He was nervous as he knew she was expecting the surgery to be successful and to see her husband alive. Suleiman's children hadn't gone to the hospital because they were too afraid and nervous.

The doctor came out of the operating room and called the receptionist to ask her to take Aisha to his office. The receptionist called Aisha and she was still nervous, she asked her whether the surgery was successful but the receptionist told her that she still had no information regarding the surgery but the doctor would like to meet her in his office. Aisha was still anxious and the receptionist took her to the doctor's office. As soon as she entered, she noticed that the doctor looked sad and nervous. She panicked and started asking him many questions:

Doctor what's happening?

Where is my husband?

Is he well?

Was the surgery successful? Tell me something…

The doctor kept quiet for a few minutes and kindly asked her to sit on the office chair. Aisha refused to sit and continued to ask the same questions to the doctor. The doctor finally convinced her to sit on the office chair and told her the sad news, "Madam, my team and I did our best to save your husband, but I regret to inform you that he didn't survive his liver cancer surgery."

Aisha screamed and replied, "no doctor, it's not possible, my husband is still alive, you must be kidding! I want to see my husband now." Then she burst into tears. The doctor tried to comfort her and took her to the operating room to show her that her husband had truly passed away. As soon as Aisha entered the operating room, she saw her husband lying in the surgery bed and noticed that he was truly dead.

She screamed again and tried to wake her husband up as she couldn't believe he was dead. But the doctor's team held her back and asked her to wait outside. Aisha was inconsolable and couldn't stop crying at the hospital. She thought the surgery would be successful and that her husband would still be alive but unfortunately it was the complete opposite. It was so sad that the doctor and other people at the hospital also cried.

Aisha called her children on the phone to announce to them that their father didn't survive the surgery and had passed away. They all rushed to the hospital to confirm whether it was really true. Awa was also at the hospital and all of them saw their father lying in the surgery bed and they all burst into tears. Awa was more affected than others because she was going through depression. She was extremely sad and decided to commit suicide this time. She couldn't bear all the pain any longer. As her family members were crying at the hospital because of Suleiman's death, Awa grabbed a knife and wanted to commit suicide. Luckily, the hospital security guard saw her and was able to stop her from hurting herself. He took the knife from her and threw it away. When Aisha and her siblings saw what had happened, they all ran to Awa and told her not to commit suicide as it wasn't worth doing that. Awa didn't want to talk to her siblings as they had all rejected her when she lost her job. Aisha was able to calm Awa down and they all left the hospital around 6am. They continued to mourn for Suleiman at home.

Awa was even more depressed and said, "why me? What have I done to deserve all this? I lost my job, my best friend and now my father." Aisha tried to comfort her and told her to stay strong. Two weeks later, the family did a funeral service for the late Suleiman and Aisha gave a speech during the service. She spoke about how great her late husband had been and the impact he had on her life and her family. She did mention that Suleiman had been a wise man, a good father and husband. She said he wasn't rich but he had always worked hard to be able to take care of his family. Her speech was so touching and inspiring and everyone clapped for her; and Suleiman was buried afterwards. Soraya and her uncle heard about Suleiman's death but didn't attend the funeral service. Soraya still hadn't forgiven Awa, and Jeremiah didn't like Suleiman because of the incident that had happened before in front of his house. He thought

Suleiman was one of the reasons why Carole divorced him since he reported him to her. Soraya and her uncle were still holding grudges against Awa and her late father. Soraya was still thinking that Awa was in a relationship with her uncle, that Jeremiah didn't forcefully kiss her and Awa was the reason why Carole divorced him. Nonetheless, Carole attended Suleiman's funeral service. She didn't hold grudges against Awa and believed that the only cause of her divorce was Jeremiah. She believed that Jeremiah forcefully kissed Awa and wanted to get into a relationship with her. She liked Awa and still considered her as her daughter. However, she couldn't convince Soraya that Awa was innocent and was rather a good person.

Aisha decided to sell Suleiman's house and used the money to buy another house because the house reminded her a lot of all the good moments she had spent with him in there when he was alive and this made her feel even sadder. She wanted to move to a new place to forget him and start a new life. She also thought that moving to a new house will benefit Awa as her depression got worse since she lost her father. Awa had been depressed for a year and her mother was really worried about it. She took her to a mental health professional on several occasions but nothing seemed to have changed. Aisha and Awa moved to a different area called "2 Plateaux Les Perles 2" and they lived in a 2-bedroom house, but Aisha still had her saloon in Yopougon.

I know the story is sad but I hope you are enjoying it so far. Let's move to Part 3.

Part 3

Awa Overcomes Depression

Aisha continued to help Awa fight her depression and was willing to do everything she could for Awa to overcome it. She always cooked for Awa even though Awa still had no appetite. She spent less time at work to be able to look after Awa at home and keep her company. Awa's siblings visited their mother from time to time but were still rejecting Awa and seemed not to care about her depression. Their mother thought that Suleiman's death and Awa's suicide attempt would draw them close to Awa but no, nothing seemed to have changed. They were still ungrateful to Awa and were not showing any love or kindness to her. This made Awa feel more depressed. She was still wondering why her siblings were acting this way towards her and couldn't believe that they weren't even helping her fight her depression. They didn't even check up on her. They went to their mother's house just to chat and eat. However,

Aisha advised them to be grateful to Awa, treat her with love, care, kindness and show empathy to her, but they were not following her advice. Their behavior was unbelievable. The only close person Awa had was her mother. Awa was very grateful to her mother for taking care of her and thanked her all the time. Moreover, the antidepressants were not working for Awa, therefore, the mental health professional gave Aisha another method to help Awa overcome her depression. He asked Aisha to help Awa make new friends.

According to the mental health professional, Awa would be able to overcome her depression if she made new friends. But the problem was that she was feeling too depressed to make friends. She still spent all her time in her room and didn't want to go out and socialise. She was still thinking about her late father, Soraya, her job loss, and how her siblings had rejected her. Although she moved to a new place, she was still the same and was hopeless. She thought her life was miserable and that she would never be happy. Her mother asked her to go out and make new friends in their new area but she said she just wanted to be alone and didn't have enough energy to reach out to others or even come out of her room. In addition, Awa didn't feel like others wanted to befriend her and felt shy to talk to other people. She thought she would not be good company. Therefore, she preferred to stay in her room and isolate herself. She even told her mental health professional that she had trouble making friends and he advised Aisha to invite people into her house so that Awa could make friends from home.

Aisha thought it was a good idea, therefore, she decided to invite one of her friends to her house. Her friend was called Naomi and had two children, a son and a daughter. Her son was called Joel, he was a businessman and his sister was called Grace, she was a nurse. Joel was one year older than Awa. Aisha asked Naomi to come to her house with her children so that they will befriend Awa in order to help her overcome her depression. Naomi agreed to come to Aisha's house with Joel and Grace. Naomi spoke to her children about Awa's depression before they went to Aisha's house and asked them to befriend her because she was feeling lonely. Naomi and her children arrived at Aisha's house and Awa was in her room at that time. They were all sitting in the living room and Aisha went to Awa's room to ask her to come to the living room to meet Naomi's children. Awa didn't want to come out of her room as she had no energy but Aisha was able to convince her.

A few minutes after, Awa went to the living room and met Joel and Grace. Joel and Grace introduced themselves to Awa and she wanted to go back to her room after meeting them, but Aisha asked her to stay in the living room to socialise with them. Awa agreed and sat next to them. Joel tried to have a conversation with Awa but she was being very brief. She was giving him short replies when he was asking her some questions. The conversation sounded like:

Joel: "how are you?"

Awa: "good."

Joel: "okay… How was your day?"

Awa: "fine."

Joel: "have you eaten?"

Awa: "yes."

Joel: "Is everything okay?"

Awa: "no."

Awa wasn't really interested in talking to Joel and this made him feel bad. He really wanted to have a proper conversation with her but it wasn't the case. Grace tried to befriend Awa and converse with her but Awa behaved similarly towards her. She gave her short replies and didn't seem interested in talking to her either. Naomi and Aisha were quite disappointed as they had thought Awa would be happy to see Joel and Grace and befriend them. Afterwards, Awa went back to her room and was still feeling depressed. Joel and Grace told their mother that they did their best to befriend Awa but it didn't work out. They said that Awa wasn't friendly to them and didn't seem to like them. Aisha told them that Awa was a good person and used to be very friendly until she became depressed. She said that they shouldn't take it personally that she was behaving this way due to her depression.

Aisha was a patient woman and never gave up on Awa. She told Naomi to come back the following week with her children. Joel and Grace didn't want to come back because they thought Awa would behave similarly but her mother convinced them to come with her the following week. Aisha still had hope that Awa was going to change and that Joel and Grace were going to befriend her. She strongly believed that Awa would be able to overcome her depression by making new friends. When Naomi and her children left the house on that day, Aisha went to talk to Awa and told her to be friendly to Joel and Grace, that they were really nice and wanted to befriend her. Aisha advised her for many hours and Awa finally agreed with her and promised her to be friendly to

Joel and Grace next time. Aisha hugged her and was excited about it.

The following week, Naomi and her children went back to Aisha's house. Awa was eating in her room when they arrived and she joined them in the living room afterwards. Surprisingly, she was happy to see them and went to hug each of them. All of them were surprised at Awa's behavior and couldn't believe what was happening. Aisha was very happy to see her daughter in a good mood. Awa began to chat with Joel and Grace and was very friendly to them this time. Awa wanted to know everything and anything about them. Joel and Grace were happy and astonished at the same time. They talked for about 3 hours and had a drink together afterwards. They even watched TV together. Awa told them the full version of her story. She told them that she had a best friend before who helped her get a job at a tailor shop, that she even got promoted to a manager's role, she financially supported her family and helped her mother start a hairdressing business but she lost her best friend, her job and became depressed, and her siblings started rejecting her, and that she also lost her father. Joel and Grace were deeply touched by her story and showed empathy to her. They told her that she should forget about her past even though it was hard and move on with her life. They promised her they will always be there for her and they all hugged each other. Aisha and Naomi were happy to see their children becoming friends and said that their friendship will help Awa overcome her depression. They exchanged their phone numbers and Joel suggested they go to the cinema on the weekend. Awa accepted the invitation and thought it was a good idea. Naomi and her children left Aisha's house late in the evening and went home. Aisha was proud of Awa and encouraged her to stay in touch with Joel and Grace. Awa went to bed afterwards and was able to sleep soundly.

Remember, Awa had insomnia before she met Joel and Grace. This was a good sign and her mother was glad that she was able to sleep well. The following morning, Aisha cooked breakfast for Awa and she was able to eat properly. This was an improvement as she didn't have an appetite before. Aisha became more optimistic and Awa told her that she was feeling better and was recovering from her depression.

The weekend arrived and Joel and Grace went to Awa's place to pick her up to go to the cinema. Awa dressed up and went to the cinema with them. She was glad to meet them and they all watched a movie together and had a lot of fun. After watching the movie, they went to an Ivorian restaurant to eat fried plantains and braised fish, a very popular dish in Ivory coast. You should definitely try it one day, it's so tasty… As they were eating, Grace said something unexpected to Joel and Awa. She said, "oh, I think you two would make a cute couple." Joel and Awa stared into each other's eyes and smiled. They pretended they didn't hear what Grace said and changed the subject. After eating, Grace and Joel dropped Awa off at her house and went back home. Joel told Grace that Awa is a nice girl and he thinks he has feelings for her. Grace was so happy to hear that and teased him. She told him she knew he has feelings for her and that's why she said the two of them would make a nice couple when they were at the restaurant. Grace told him that she thinks Awa likes him too but she's not totally sure about it, therefore, she will talk to her to confirm it.

After a while, Awa was completely healed from her depression. She could eat more, sleep better and was able to do everything she could do before she became depressed. She was even looking prettier and better. She had more energy and became proactive. Aisha was so happy about it and immediately called the mental health professional to tell him about it. He rejoiced and congratulated Aisha for always being with Awa throughout her depression. Awa told him that she overcame her depression when she made new friends and thanked him for all his support and advice. Aisha called Naomi to tell her that Awa completely recovered from her depression and invited her and her children to her home to celebrate it. Joel and Grace were also happy to hear that Awa had overcome her depression. They all went to Aisha's house to celebrate it and Aisha told them that Awa overcame her depression when she became friends with Joel and Grace. She thanked them and gave them gifts. Joel and Grace congratulated Awa and wished her the best of luck in her endeavors. Awa thanked them as well and was really grateful to them.

As they were celebrating, Joel asked Awa whether she would like to work and Awa said yes. Joel told her that his father has a clothing shop and was looking for a manager to manage it. Awa was astonished and couldn't believe what was happening, she thought she was dreaming. She asked him whether he was serious and Joel said, "yes, I am serious. If you want to work, I can ask my father to employ you in his clothing shop as a manager."

Aisha was also astonished. Then Awa said, "yes Joel, I accept the offer, I would be glad to work at your father's clothing shop as a manager. I was the manager of a tailor shop before so I have effective managerial skills." Joel immediately called his father on the phone to prove to Awa that he was being serious, and he told him that he found someone who can work as the manager of his clothing shop. He told him about Awa and said that she had the skills required for the job. His father agreed to employ her and asked him to tell her that she was going to start her new job the following week then he hung up the phone. Joel told Awa what his father told him on the phone and she was so excited and couldn't stop thanking him. She said, "Joel, you are an angel. Since I met you, my life has changed, I overcame my depression and now I have a new job." Joel told her that he will always be there for her. He further told her that she will earn 1,500,000 CFA francs a month at the clothing shop and Awa was even happier and shed tears of joy. She completely forgot about her past and was willing to move on and start her new life. Aisha thanked Joel and his family.

The following day, Grace asked Awa whether she liked Joel and she began to smile and said, "yes." Grace was happy to hear that and told her that Joel liked her too and the two of them should get into a relationship. Awa told her that she didn't know how to go about it, she was too shy to tell Joel that she liked him. Grace told her not to worry about it and that she was going to handle it. Afterwards, Grace asked Joel to invite Awa to a restaurant for dinner and tell her that he likes her and would like to get into a relationship with her. Joel was a bit afraid and asked her whether Awa told her that she liked him. Grace acted as if Awa didn't tell her anything and she told him to be confident and just invite her for dinner. Joel invited Awa to a classy restaurant and she accepted the invitation with pleasure.

Two days later, Joel went to pick her up to go to the restaurant and as they were eating, he told her that he liked her. Awa couldn't stop smiling and kept on staring into his eyes. She was so happy and told him that she liked him too. Joel was glad to hear that and they both kissed each other at the table. It was so romantic. As if it wasn't enough, Joel proposed to her. Awa was a bit afraid as she didn't expect that at all. She kept quiet for a few minutes and said, "yes."

Joel rejoiced and hugged her tightly. He then dropped her off at home afterwards and told Grace about everything that happened at the restaurant. Grace was shocked as she didn't know he was going to propose to her, she just thought he was going to ask her to get into a relationship with him. But no! Joel wanted to marry Awa... He told her that Awa said that she liked him and said yes to his marriage proposal. Grace was happy for the two of them and called Awa to hear more about the story.

Awa told her about what happened at the restaurant and confirmed that she agreed to marry Joel. She also told her mother about it. Aisha was shocked and couldn't believe it. She congratulated Awa and was so proud of her. She told her that her father would be proud of her if he was still alive. She agreed with Awa's decision and wished her the best of luck. She further advised her on how she should behave as a wife. Joel told his parents that he was going to get married to Awa, and they were proud of him and excited about it. Naomi immediately called Aisha to discuss it. Aisha also called Awa's siblings to tell them that Awa overcame her depression, found a new job and was going to get married soon. They were all shocked as they thought Awa would never be able to overcome her depression and achieve anything in life. Remember, they all rejected her when she was depressed. They all felt ashamed of themselves and went to Aisha's house to apologise to Awa. Awa forgave them and told them that she was really disappointed in them when they all rejected her. They apologised again and she asked them to forget about the past and move on.

Awa started her new job at the clothing shop and really liked it. She worked very hard and Joel's father was happy with her performance. He didn't regret hiring her and told Joel that she's been doing a great job. Moreover, Joel and Awa planned to marry in two months.

One day, Awa received a phone call from Soraya and was so surprised. She didn't really expect her call at all. She thought Soraya would never reach out to her or forgive her. Soraya was feeling shy and guilty on the phone as she had not been talking to Awa for a long time. She was even stuttering while Awa kept quiet and was listening to her. Soraya asked her how she was doing and where she lived. Remember, both of them had not been talking since Awa lost her job. Awa gave her short replies as she was still disappointed in her for abandoning her. Soraya told Awa that she believed

Jeremiah forcefully kissed her and that she was innocent. She apologised to her and asked her to meet up. Awa asked her to give her some time to think about it, that she was really hurt when Soraya didn't believe her and abandoned her. She told her that she should have trusted her and that best friends are supposed to trust each other. She further told her how she suffered from her job loss, became depressed and attempted suicide. She also added that she was disappointed not to see her at her father's funeral. Soraya didn't even call Awa to offer condolences when Suleiman passed away. Awa told her that she never thought that their friendship was going to end. Soraya began to cry on the phone and apologised again. But Awa told her that she met new friends and she didn't want to suffer again. She wasn't sure whether it would be a good idea to be friends with Soraya again so, she told her she was going to think about it then she hung up the phone. Awa called Grace to tell her that her ex best friend had called her to apologise that she didn't know what to do and felt like she should not be friends with her. Grace asked Awa to forgive Soraya and be friends with her again. Awa agreed with Grace and said she was going to forgive her but wouldn't be close to her like before. She didn't want to get hurt again and go through the same pain. Grace told her that she made the right choice. A few days after, Awa called Soraya to tell her that she had forgiven her and they could be friends again but not best friends. She told her that Grace was now her best friend and that they loved each other so much. Soraya was quite disappointed that Awa had a new best friend but was happy to have her back as her friend. Furthermore, Awa told her that she was going to get married soon and invited her to her wedding. Soraya was surprised and agreed to come to her wedding.

Joel and Awa got married and their family members and friends were all at the wedding celebrating with them. It was a memorable day in Awa's life and Aisha was overwhelmed with happiness and shed tears of joy. She was a wonderful mother who loved her child and never gave up on her. She had fought really hard to help Awa overcome her depression and she's a great role model to all mothers all over the world. Joel and Awa moved to a beautiful house in Cocody. They were happily married and planned to have kids together. Awa and Grace remained best friends for life.

Awa won her battle with Depression!

Depression is a serious problem, but the good news is that every problem has a solution. And Awa's story demonstrates that receiving support from the people who love you and making friends can help overcome depression.

End of the Story!

Lightning Source UK Ltd.
Milton Keynes UK
UKHW010645090820
367908UK00001B/60